Geronimo

THE JOURNEY THROUGH TIME

DINOSAUR DISASTER

Scholastic Inc.

ISBN 978-0-545-61127-5

Based on an original idea by Elisabetta Dami.

www.geronimostilton.com

Published by Scholastic Inc., 557 Broadway, New York, NY 10012.
SCHOLASTIC and associated logos are trademarks and/or registered trademarks of Scholastic Inc.

Stilton is the name of a famous English cheese. It is a registered trademark of the Stilton Cheese Makers' Association. For more information, go to www.stiltoncheese.com.

Text by Geronimo Stilton
Original title *Viaggio nel tempo*
Cover by Silvia Bigolin (pencils and inks) and Christian Aliprandi (color)
Illustration concepts by Lorenzo Chiavini, Blasco Pisapia, Roberto Ronchi, and Valeria Turati
Illustration production by Silvia Bigolin, Danilo Barozzi, Valeria Brambilla, Giuseppe Guindani (pencils and inks), Christian Aliprandi (color), and Francesco Barbieri (appendix)
Graphics by Merenguita Gingermouse, Zeppola Zap, and Yuko Egusa with Chiara Cebraro and Studio Editoriale Littera

Special thanks to AnnMarie Anderson
Translated by Lidia Tramontozzi
Interior design by Kay Petronio

12 11 10 9 8 7 6 5 4 3   13 14 15 16 17 18/0

Printed in the U.S.A.   40

This edition first printing, September 2013

TRAVELERS ON
THE JOURNEY THROUGH TIME

Dear rodent friends,
My name is Stilton, *Geronimo Stilton*. I am
the editor and publisher of *The Rodent's Gazette*,
the most famous newspaper on Mouse Island.
I'm about to tell you the story of one of my most
amazing adventures. Let me introduce you to the
other mice you will meet. . . .

THEA STILTON

My sister, Thea, is a special correspondent for
The Rodent's Gazette. She is very athletic and
one of the most stubborn and determined mice
I have ever met!

BENJAMIN

My nephew Benjamin is the
sweetest and most affectionate
little mouselet in the whole world.

TRAP

My cousin Trap is an incredible
prankster. His favorite pastime
is playing jokes on me.

PROFESSOR PAWS VON VOLT

Professor von Volt is a genius inventor
who has dedicated his life to making
amazing new discoveries. This time,
he built a time machine!

THE MYSTERIOUS LETTER

It was a FOGGY December morning. I left home, got a coffee at a nearby café, and munched on a **cheesy** croissant as I leafed through my newspaper, *The Rodent's Gazette*, while walking to work. Five minutes later, I was in my office.

I immediately noticed a **mysterious** letter sitting on my desk. The envelope was **sealed** with a yellow wax stamp with a peculiar symbol on it: a **QUESTION MARK**.

The handwriting looked **very** familiar to me. I opened the

Geronimo Stilton

envelope cautiously. A **rusty** key slipped out along with a sheet of **crumbly** old notepaper that smelled like **moldy** cheese.

Intrigued, I read the note.

Mr. Geronimo Stilton
Editor of *The Rodent's Gazette*
17 Swiss Cheese Center
New Mouse City, Mouse Island
12121

a mysterious letter . . . a mysterious letter . . .
A mysterious letter . . .

Geronimo!

Take the number 17 trolley from Romano Square and get off at the seventh stop. Walk to the traffic light, then take the second street on the left, then the third on the right, and then the first on the left. Cross the bridge, take twenty-three-and-a-half steps until you reach the billboard with the gorgonzola cheese ad. Then take fourteen steps toward the telephone booth. You should find yourself standing in front of a clock. Turn your back to the clock and take seven steps toward the pizzeria. Go inside the pizzeria, walk to the bathroom, exit through the small window, and climb over the low wall.

Now walk for exactly thirty seconds toward the shoe store, go around the corner, and continue walking until you see a little black door with a sign on it that says DO NOT ENTER. Open the door using the enclosed key. Go through the door, and you'll find yourself in an alley. Take the first right, then the second left, then the third right. Turn into a yard and proceed until you reach a large Dumpster. Climb into the Dumpster for an amazing adventure!

Signed,
??????

P.S. Commit these instructions to memory, then destroy the letter! Do not talk about this to anyone! It's an extremely secretive secret!

"Moldy mozzarella!" I squeaked. "An adventure in a Dumpster? What an **intriguing** letter!"

I carefully reread the letter and examined it with a magnifying glass.

"Hmmm," I said to myself. "It *could* be a prank, but if it's not . . ."

I thought about it for a minute as my whiskers trembled with excitement. Then I made my decision. I memorized the instructions, tore the letter into a thousand pieces, and without saying anything to anyone, quietly slipped out of the office. I **scampered** to the corner, crossed the street, and ran to catch the **number 17** trolley.

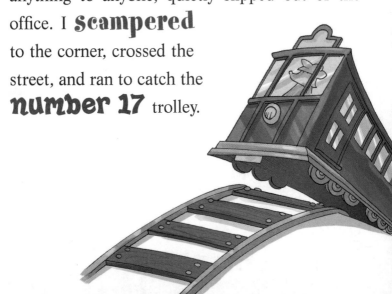

MY WHISKERS TREMBLED . . .

The trolley was very, very **CROWDED**. I pushed my way through rats and mice on their way to work. I looked out the window. A dusting of fresh **SNOW** covered the streets of New Mouse City, and it was truly **BEAUTIFUL**! The rooftops looked like white pillows, while the **ice** made the trees look like they were dressed for a party in delicate *lace*.

Lost in thought, I almost didn't notice the trolley had come to the seventh stop. The doors creaked open. **Creak! Creak!**

I stepped off the trolley to find that the **FOG** had gotten thicker. I couldn't see anything beyond my own paw! I cleaned my fogged glasses and tried to remember the instructions in the **MYSTERIOUS** letter.

Oh, right! I had to walk to the **traffic light**! I took the second street on the left, then the third on the right, and then the first on the left. I crossed the **bridge** and counted

twenty-three-and-a-half steps toward the **GORGONZOLA** cheese billboard.

I counted **fourteen** steps toward the phone booth. There was the **CLOCK**! After counting **SEVEN** steps, I found myself in front of the pizzeria. I went in. The owner

GORGONZOLA CHEESE

YUMMY!

If you don't try it, you won't know what you're missing!

winked at me. **HOW STRANGE!** I went into the **BATHROOM**, exited through the small window, and climbed over the low wall.

I walked for exactly **thirty** seconds toward

RESTROOMS

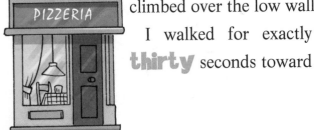

PIZZERIA

the shoe store. I went around the corner, and I found a small black door with a sign that read **DO NOT ENTER**.

I opened the door using the **MYSTERIOUS** key, and I found myself in an **ALLEY**. I took the first right, then the second left, then the third right, and finally turned into a **YARD**. There, I found the Dumpster. I took off the lid. Ugh! 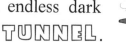 **What a stench!** I pinched my nose and climbed inside. But as soon as I got in, the bottom gave out and I fell into what seemed to be an endless dark **TUNNEL**.

I shouted as loudly as I could:

"HEEEEEEEEEEEEEEELP!"
"HEEEEEEEEEEEEELP!"

Everything around me was **PITCH-BLACK**. I fell for what seemed like forever. Was it seconds, minutes, or hours? I couldn't tell. I only know that at one point I **BOUNCED** onto some sort of trampoline. Boing! I bounced! And bounced! And bounced!

A steel clamp grabbed my tail. Then I heard a mechanical voice repeat over and over again:

"Is it him, or isn't it him? Is it him, or isn't it him? Is it him, or isn't it him?"

A little robot quickly slid toward me and began to sniff at my fur. SNIFF! SNIFF! SNIFF!

"It's him!" the robot exclaimed. "It's Geronimo Stinton!"

Even though I was SUSPENDED in midair, I found the strength to correct the tiny machine.

"Excuse me, my name is Stilton, *Geronimo Stilton*!" I insisted.

Suddenly, the steel clamp on my tail released and I fell to the floor with a *thud*. I looked up just as a small door flew open. I instantly recognized a **familiar** snout.

"Professor von Volt!" I exclaimed. "What are you doing here?"

THE FORMULA FOR
TIME TRAVEL

Professor von Volt and I have been friends for a long time. He's a **FASCINATING** mouse who has devoted his life to making new scientific **discoveries**. Unfortunately, I never know where to find him. That's because he has a habit of constantly moving his **SECRET** lab without telling anyone because he doesn't want other mice to know what he's working on! That means he usually has to **seek** me out when he needs my help with one of his projects or **experiments**.

"Geronimo!" he **EXCLAIMED**, giving me a

PROFESSOR PAWS VON VOLT

big hug. "What do you think of my new lab?"

I looked around the huge subterranean room. In front of me was a big steel desk covered in glass TEST TUBES and beakers. Each one was filled with a mysterious COLORED liquid. The test tubes bubbled and emitted a variety of stinky vapors. I also noticed several sheets of paper covered with sketches and scientific FORMULAS.

"Geronimo, I sent you that MYSTERIOUS letter because I wanted to be sure no one could figure out where my laboratory is," the professor explained. "But I wanted you to come here so that I could show you my latest and greatest iNveNtioN!"

"A new invention?" I asked, intrigued.

"Yes!" the professor squeaked with excitement. "It's a machine that allows mice to TRAVEL THROUGH TIME!"

He pointed to a MYSTERIOUS object in the center of the room that was covered with a sheet.

Here it is . . . the time machine!

To open, press the first letter *M*

Mouse Mover 3000, the time machine

"You mean it's a *time machine*?" I asked, amazed.

Professor von Volt lifted the sheet off the object to reveal a brass time machine shaped liked an **ENORMOUSE** slice of cheese. An engraving on it read: MOUSE MOVER 3000.

"This time machine can travel *forward* and **BACKWARD** in time," the professor explained. "It can also move in and out of **PARALLEL WORLDS** like a Möbius strip."

Möbius strip

I looked inside the time machine: It had a bright BRASS finish with solid bolts. I noticed five velvet-backed chairs that looked like dentist's chairs, except they were equipped with sturdy **SAFETY BELTS**.

Professor von Volt explained that to travel,

THE MYSTERIOUS MÖBIUS STRIP

This fascinating play-experiment makes us think of the three dimensions and of the mystery of parallel worlds. The German mathematician and astronomer August Ferdinand Möbius (1790–1868) discovered the Möbius Strip in 1858.

∞ is the shape of the Möbius strip and the symbol for infinity in mathematics.

Take a strip of paper and color each side a different color.

Take a strip of paper . . .

Twist the strip as shown and glue it as indicated. Is the purple side on the inside or the outside? How about the yellow side? Notice that the strip only has one side and one edge. If you trace your finger along the length of the strip, your finger will return to the starting point without crossing the edge of the strip.

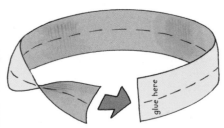

glue here

. . . twist it and glue it . . .

. . . and cut it down the middle!

Now cut the strip down the middle. Surprise! The strip doesn't break into two pieces. Instead, it becomes an even longer strip with another twist in it.

one only had to program the **CHRONOMETER**, which was a super-advanced timepiece, with where and when to visit!

Right next to the Chronometer was a red button labeled **PRESS HERE**.

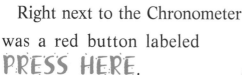

PROFESSOR VON VOLT continued to explain how the time machine worked.

"Geronimo, do you know about Albert Einstein's **THEORY OF RELATIVITY**?" he asked me.

"Well, I learned it in school, but . . ." My snout turned purple with embarrassment. I didn't

Albert Einstein (1879–1955)
Albert Einstein was a German physicist. His theory of relativity explained the important link between space and time using the formula $E=mc^2$. Einstein's work helped launch a new era in theoretical physics.

remember a **THING** about Einstein's theory!

"Well, in Einstein's formula E=mc², **energy** is equal to **MASS** times the **SPEED OF LIGHT** squared, right?" the professor asked.

"Yes, of course," I replied.

"One evening I decided to take a **warm** bath," Professor von Volt continued. "I grabbed a cube of **cheese** to snack on as I soaked. I **GNAWED** it quickly, and it disappeared in an instant. The cheese was transferred to another dimension — my **STOMACH**! Suddenly, I developed a new formula:

$$E = (mc)(vmg)^3$$

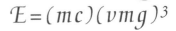

*Energy = the **mass** of the **cheese** times the **velocity** at which the **mouse gnawed** it, **cubed**!*

"When I did some calculations using my new formula, I discovered it was possible to travel though **time**!" the professor continued. "I'm leaving on my first journey as **SOON** as possible, and I need some passengers for the **MOUSE MOVER 3000**. Would you and your family like to come?"

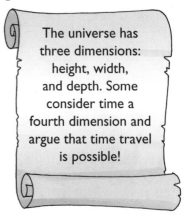

The universe has three dimensions: height, width, and depth. Some consider time a fourth dimension and argue that time travel is possible!

"M-m-me?" I squeaked. "Oh, no, Professor, I couldn't."

Suddenly, Thea's and Trap's faces **POPPED** into my mind. I knew the two of them would **love** to go on a trip through time. I sighed. I couldn't say no.

"Professor, the Stilton family would be **honored** to travel with you!" I told him.

I'LL BE RIGHT THERE!

Geronimo Stilton

I called *The Rodent's Gazette*. My sister, Thea, answered the phone.

"Can you keep a **secret**?" I WHiSPeReD. "Professor von Volt invented a **time machine** and invited us to travel with him. Get your things ready, and meet me as soon as you can!"

"Let me grab my **CAMERA**, and I'll be right there!" she shouted. "What a **FABUMOUSE** scoop!"

Thea Stilton

"Shhh!" I said. "Talk softly. Somebody might hear you!"

"I won't whisper a **SQUEAK** to anyone,"
Thea promised. "I give you my
rodent's word! I'll pass
you on to Trap."

Trap Stilton

A moment later, Trap got on
the phone.

"What's this about a **TRIP**
with the professor?" he shouted.
"Look, I'll come only if there's
going to be some decent **food**!"

"***Shhh!***" I said frantically.
"Please don't **YELL**! It's a secret! A super-
classified secret!"

"Okay, okay," he grumbled. "I'll come. But
if there's a treasure involved, I want my share!
Rodent's word, okay?"

"Yes, yes, yes," I agreed **HURRIEDLY**.
"We'll talk about it later. In the meantime, get
here on the double. We're about to **leave**."

"It's a deal!" Trap replied. "But first, I want to try out a new joke on you."

"Okay, okay," I agreed. "But **HURRY**!"

"What did the mouse say when the cat bit his tail?" he asked.

"Hmmm . . . er . . . gee . . . well, it depends how BIG the cat is. . . ." I said.

"Gerry Berry, you have no sense of humor!" Trap groaned.

"Trap!" I complained. "You know I hate it when you call me that."

Trap handed the phone to my nephew Benjamin, who giggled.

Benjamin Stilton

"Uncle, the MOUSE said, 'That's the end of me!'" he squeaked. "Get it?"

I **chuckled** at the joke.

"Is it true?" Benjamin asked once he stopped laughing.

"Are you really going to **TRAVEL** through time? Please, please take me along!"

"I'd **love** to take you, Benjamin," I explained, "but it could be a very **DANGEROUS** trip!"

"It won't be **DANGEROUS** if I'm with you, Uncle," Benjamin replied. "I know you'll protect me. Please take me, Uncle. **Pretty please?!**"

I sighed. I can never say no to Benjamin.

"Okay, my little morsel of **cheese**," I agreed with a smile. "You can come, too!"

"Thank you, Uncle!" he **squeaked**. "Thank you, thank you! You're the **best** uncle in the world!"

He handed the phone back to Thea, and I told her how to find Professor von Volt's **SECRET** laboratory.

Half an hour later, I heard the sound of the **GONG**.

Thea, Trap, and Benjamin had arrived!

I heard the sound of the gong . . . . Bonggggggg Bonggggggg Bonggggggg Bonggggggg

SAUSAGE FOR DINOSAURS

Professor von Volt opened a little refrigerator.

"I've been saving this bottle for years," he explained. "I've been waiting for a special occasion, and this is it!"

Trap examined the bottle with a knowing air.

"Phew," my cousin whistled. He was obviously

Photo taken by Thea

impressed. "This is a milkshake made of French Roquefort cheese from 1958. It's **veeeerrry** expensive! And I'll bet it's **WHISKER-LICKING** good. You have very good taste, Professor."

Thea took a group PHOTO as Benjamin shook the professor's paw.

"And now, let's go over a few **SAFETY** precautions," the professor told us.

"FIRST: The Chronometer must always be programmed with your desired destination. Be very careful! If you enter the wrong information, we could get lost in time!"

Holey cheese! I would be extremely careful. I didn't want to get lost in time!

The professor took something out of his pocket.

"SECOND: You'll need earplugs because the trip will be rather noisy."

He handed out the earplugs.

"By the way, does anyone get airsick?" he asked.

"Geronimo gets airsick, seasick, train sick, bus sick, and even taxi sick," Trap *SNICKERED*.

"Hmmm," the professor said. "Well, then, dear Geronimo, you'll probably experience a little *nausea*. But don't worry. Each trip takes exactly **Sixty Seconds** — no more, no less!

"**THIRD**: The past cannot be modified in any way, shape, or form, or it will change the future with disastrous consequences!

TRAVEL NECESSITIES:

compass

remote control for the Chronometer

first aid kit

matches

needle and thread

Swiss Army knife

water

sleeping bag and mattress

fishing line

cheese

crackers

chocolate

"**FOURTH**: Keep my *Time Travel Survival Manual* handy at all times."

Time Travel Survival Manual

He waved the manual at us.

"This could **SAVE** your life!" he shouted. "For example, if you encounter a dinosaur, check the manual to find out if it's an **HERBIVORE** or a **CARNIVORE**! If it's a carnivore, you'd better run as fast as you can!"

YIKES!

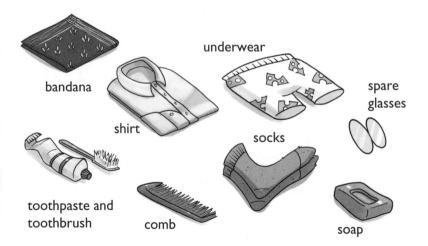

bandana

underwear

spare glasses

shirt

socks

toothpaste and toothbrush

comb

soap

Then Professor von Volt became even more **SERIOUS**.

"Our secret journey through time has three **objectives**," he told us.

• In the **prehistoric period**: Find out why dinosaurs became extinct.

• In **ancient Egypt**: Find out how Cheops, the Great Pyramid of Giza, was built!

• In **medieval England**: Uncover the secrets of King Arthur and his court!

I had to remember everything about the **amazing** adventure I was about to take.

So I slipped a plastic envelope containing my **TRAVEL JOURNAL** and *pencil* into my pocket.

Meanwhile, Trap muttered, "What if we never make it back? We could become **sausage** for dinosaurs! Or a pharaoh might bury us alive in a giant **SARCOPHAGUS**! Or we might end up **skewered** like mouse kebabs on a medieval knight's sword!"

"Don't worry!" Benjamin piped up confidently. "Uncle Geronimo will **PROTECT** us."

He looked at me with such hope in his eyes. **Moldy mozzarella!** I really, really hoped I could live up to my dear nephew's expectations.

A Mysterious Blue Fog

I climbed into the *time machine* first. Trap, Thea, Benjamin, and the professor were still gathering their things.

"Would you please pass me the compass, the remote control for the CHRONOMETER, and the first aid kit?" I asked Trap.

"Sure thing, Cuz," Trap replied. Then he began

Oooooops!

to **juggle** the three objects in the air.

I shook my head in **DISMAY**. Why, oh, why did my cousin have to be such a jokester?

Suddenly, Trap **TRIPPED** over one of the many stacks of books and papers Professor von Volt had around his lab.

The **COMPASS** went flying into the dashboard. **CRASH!**

The **remote control** bonked me in the head. **CLONK!**

And the FiRST AiD KiT hit the door of  the **MOUSE MOVER 3000**, causing it to slam shut.

THUD!

"**OUCHIE!**" I cried.

To my **horror**, I realized that the remote control had

activated the CHRONOMETER. I tried to jump out of the time machine, but the door was stuck. It was too late!

The MOUSE MOVER 3000 began spinning faster and faster.

I heard an extremely LOUD sound and understood why the professor had suggested earplugs. The little ship filled with a mysterious BLUE FOG, and I heard a huge bang.

BANGGGGGGGGGGGGGGGGG!

The time machine came to a sudden stop. Dazed, I gripped the armchair and waited for my head to stop spinning. It felt as if tiny butterflies were flying around it.

Worried, I called out to the others.

"Thea?" I shouted. "Trap? Benjamin? Professor

von Volt? Are you out there?"

No one answered.

Cautiously, I pressed the **BUTTON** to open the door.

I raised my head and looked outside.

I was
left
breathless
with
amazement!

THE JURASSIC PERIOD
199 to 145 million years ago

Ginkgo
biloba leaf

Archaeopteryx

Brachiosaurus

Ichthyosaurus

Ferns

Dryosaurus

Megazostrodon

Prehistoric
mushrooms

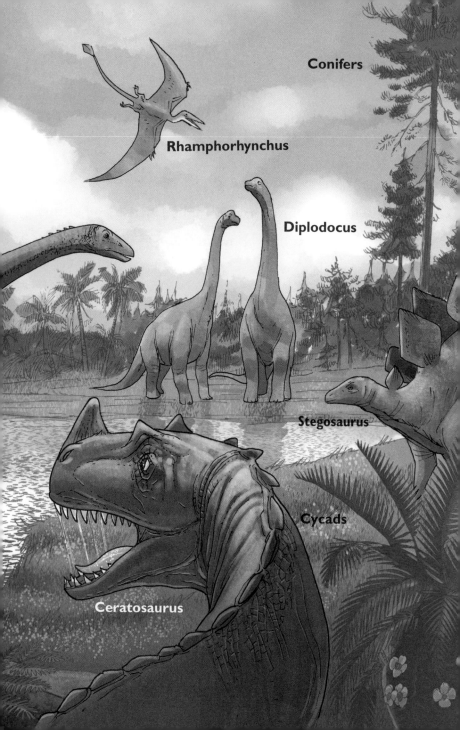

I Got Lost in Time!

It was such an awesome sight I had to pinch my tail to make sure I wasn't **DReamInG**. I saw tall flowerless trees packed with **LUSH** leaves with strange cones instead of fruit. There were **bushes** of ferns and horsetails.

Between the leaves, I saw the neck of a **DIPLODOCUS** emerge from a pond. Next to it was the armored tail of a **STEGOSAURUS**. In the distance, a volcano shot a puff of vapor into the air, and the earth trembled.

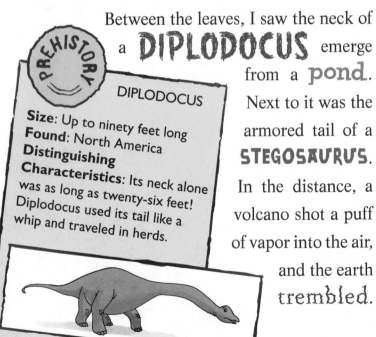

PREHISTORY

DIPLODOCUS

Size: Up to ninety feet long
Found: North America
Distinguishing Characteristics: Its neck alone was as long as twenty-six feet! Diplodocus used its tail like a whip and traveled in herds.

A flying reptile silently glided by.

I glanced at the **CHRONOMETER**:

150 million years ago
Jurassic period

I was in the **Jurassic period**, the era of the **DINOSAURS**! I tried to reprogram the **CHRONOMETER**, but it was no use. It was stuck.

Holey cheese! What was I going to do? I was going to be **DINNER** for the

PREHISTORY

STEGOSAURUS

Size: Up to thirty feet long
Found: North America
Distinguishing Characteristics: Herbivorous dinosaur that lived during the late Jurassic period. The bony plates on its back and tail arose from its skin, not its skeleton.

dinos! It was just as I had feared. I, Geronimo Stilton, was lost in time!

I shut myself inside the time machine and began to sob. "I'm alone and far away from home! I'm scared! I'm extremely scared! I'm ridiculously scared out of my mind!"

To give myself a little **courage**, I began talking to myself in a loud voice.

"Everything's fine," I shouted. "I'm going to make it!"

I repeated it **over** and **over** again.

"Of course I'm going to make it! I will make it. I will make it. I will make it!"

I picked myself up, stood up straight, and opened the porthole. Then I climbed out of the ship, took a deep breath, and entered the **prehistoric** forest.

It was humid outside and very, very **hot**. I took out my travel journal and made some notes.

Squeeeak!

Oh, why, oh, why did the **Jurassic** period have to be so hot? I was **ROASTING** like a mouse **KEBAB**! Suddenly, it became shady and cool. I breathed a sigh of relief.

"Ah, how **wonderful**!" I exclaimed. "The sky is getting cloudy, and I'll have a break from this terrible heat. . . ."

I looked up to the sky, but I had barely lifted my head when an **ENORMOUSE** Rhamphorhynchus grabbed me in its claws and **MOUSENAPPED** me!

I DON'T WANT TO BE A DINO SNACK!

"**Heeeelp!**" I squeaked. "I want to get off!"

But the Rhamphorhynchus kept on *FLYING*.

"**Holey cheese!**" I cried as the wind rushed through my fur. "This breeze is really cooling me off!"

Snap!

Snap!

Protosuchus

Ophthalmosaurus

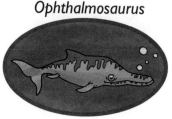

We **hovered** over a lake. Here and there among the waves swam Ophthalmosaurus, **marine** reptiles that are similar to dolphins. On the **LAKESHORE**, I saw a herd of Protosuchus, which are similar to **CROCODILES**. As we flew over, the Protosuchus raised their snouts and opened their jaws. **Snap! Snap!**

"Let me **goooooooooo**!" I shouted to the Rhamphorhynchus.

But the beast didn't listen. Then I had an idea: I reached up and **TICKLED** its belly! The creature dropped me immediately. I *PLUMMETED* down and landed on something soft.

"Ah!" I exclaimed as I massaged my sore tail. "I'm finally free!"

Then I turned to see two enormouse yellow **EYES** staring at me. *SQUEEEEEEAK!* It

was an **Allosaurus**!

I tried to think. Was Allosaurus **HERBIVOROUS** or **carnivorous**? **HERBIVOROUS** or **carnivorous**? **HERBIVOROUS** or **carnivorous**?

He opened wide his mouth, and I saw his jaws bristling with RAZOR-SHARP teeth.

"Allosaurus is **carnivoroooous**!" I yelled. "I don't want to become a dinosaur's snack! **HEEEEEEEELP!**"

I ran through the forest as *FAST* as I could.

I ran and ran and ran. Suddenly, I found myself

I don't want to become . . .

in front of a **SLAB** of rock. I was **trapped**! The Allosaurus came closer, **studying** me with mean, beady eyes. He looked **hungry**. **VERRRRY** hungry.

The **Allosaurus** took a step closer. My whiskers quivered in fear. Then I heard another **ROAR**.

ALLOSAURUS

Size: Up to forty-five feet long

Found: North America, Africa, and Australia

Distinguishing Characteristics: Allosaurus was the largest carnivorous dinosaur in the Jurassic period. Its name means "different reptile." It had more than seventy long, sharp serrated teeth and slashing claws on its small arms. It also had bony knobs and ridges on the top of its head.

...a dinosaur's snack!

PREHISTORY

MEGALOSAURUS

Size: Up to thirty feet long
Found: Europe
Distinguishing Characteristics: Megalosaurus was a carnivorous dinosaur that lived during the Jurassic period. Its name means "great lizard."

Its front claws had three fingers with slashing claws, which were designed for gripping prey.

"Roaaaaaaar!"

It was a **hungry-looking Megalosaurus**! Chewy cheddar **cheese sticks** — didn't these dinosaurs ever have a **SQUARE** meal? Then maybe they wouldn't be so interested in a tiny mouse snack like me!

I **CRAWLED** behind a tree trunk and tried to make myself very, very small.

What could be worse than one hungry dinosaur? I thought to myself. The answer: **TWO** hungry dinosaurs!

"Urgghhhhhh . . ." said the Allosaurus.

"Kkreeoookkkkkkkk!" replied the Megalosaurus.

"Gnkkkkgrrkkkkkkkkkkk!" roared the Allosaurus.

I didn't stick around to hear what the Megalosaurus had to say in reply. Instead, I ran breathlessly toward the **MOUSE MOVER 3000** and jumped inside. I closed the porthole with a slam.

The two beasts **POUNDED** on the ship, trying to get me to come out.

"Krrrrrkkkktttgnkkkkk!"

Suddenly, the **CHRONOMETER** started to buzz. Holey cheese! It had come unstuck! I was going to **escape** the Jurassic period . . . but where was I going now? I was about to find out.

BANG!

I'll Never, Ever, Ever Get Home Again!

After several hums and buzzes, the **MOUSE MOVER 3000** stopped. The CHRONOMETER read:

65 million years ago
Cretaceous period

I peeked out the porthole. I was still in **PReHISTORIC** times, but the scenery had changed. I was in the **Cretaceous period**!

First I had been mousenapped by a flying reptile, and then I almost became an Allosaurus's

CRETACEOUS PERIOD
144 to 65 million years ago

Pteranodon

Palms

Torosaurus

Saurolophus

Archelo

Dromaeosaurus

Frog

Opossum

Snail

Salamander

Magnolia

Albertosaurus

Ouranosaurus

Heron ancestor

Equisetum

Panoplosaurus

Crocodile

Snake

snack. Could anything else possibly go wrong?

Uh-oh. Thinking of how I had almost become a dino **snack** made me realize how hungry I was. My tummy grumbled and rumbled, and I would have given anything for a tiny little **morsel** of cheese.

Did they even have **cheese** during the Cretaceous period? There was only one way to find out.

I climbed out of the **MOUSE MOVER 3000** and began to search around outside for something to eat. Suddenly, I heard a **rustle** behind me. I turned just in time to see the **MOUSE MOVER 3000** spinning around and around.

An instant later, the time machine had **VANISHED**!

"Oh, no!" I sobbed. "Now I'll **NEVER, EVER, EVER** get home again!"

I'm Not Your Mother!

Just when I thought things couldn't get any worse, it started to **RAIN**. I took cover under a *ginkgo biloba* leaf and curled up inside a large abandoned nest.

I cried as I thought of my family. Would I ever hug **THEA** and **TRAP** again? And I missed **Benjamin** so much! But crying wasn't going

to get me anywhere. So I opened the professor's *Time Travel Survival Manual* and began to read by the SILVERY light of the moon. The hours flew by. At dawn, I closed the book, satisfied. I now knew everything there was to know about **PreHistoric tiMes**!

Suddenly I heard a sound.

Tap, tap, tap!

I rummaged through the nest's leaves and found a large, delicate ivory-colored **egg**.

The egg had a little **crack** in it. Suddenly, the crack began getting bigger and bigger. An odd-looking little head with two tiny surprised **EYES** popped out. The eyes looked at me in AMAZEMENT.

It was a baby Triceratops!

"Snnniiiiiiiiiiiiiick!" the baby dinosaur howled.

I found a dinosaur's egg under the leaves!

I **STOOD** up. The baby dinosaur **STOOD** up!

I **scratched** my head. He **scratched** his head!

I **JUMPED** to the left. He **JUMPED** to the left!

I **JUMPED** to the right. He **JUMPED** to the right!

Why was he imitating me? **Why? Why? Why?**

Suddenly, I **UNDERSTOOD**: The baby Triceratops thought I was his **MOTHER** because I was the first living thing he saw when he came out of his egg!

"I'm not your mother," I told him. "I'm a **MOUSE!**"

Snnniiiiiiiiiiiick!

Ediacara biota

One of the earliest forms of multicellular life, Ediacara biota lived in the Edicara Hills of Australia about 575 million years ago.

Trilobite

Insect

Amphibian

TRIASSIC PERIOD
250 to 200 million years ago

Cynognathus

Procompsognathus

JURASSIC PERIOD
199 to 145 million years ago

Ichthyosaurus

Pterosaur

Coelurus

Stegosaurus

Brachiosaurus

CRETACEOUS PERIOD
144 to 65 million years ago

Iguanadon

Corythosaurus

Tyrannosaurus

Triceratops

PROTEROZOIC EON
2.5 billion to 542 million years ago

PALEOZOIC ERA
542 to 251 million years ago

Scientists subdivide the history of
Earth into ERAS and PERIODS.
Dinosaurs developed during the
MESOZOIC ERA, which is divided
into three periods: the TRIASSIC,
JURASSIC, and CRETACEOUS.

MESOZOIC ERA
250 to 65 million years ago

*Dinosaurs appeared
around 230 million
years ago and
disappeared around
65 million years ago.*

Anchisaurus

CENOZOIC ERA
65 million years ago to today

The carnivorous dino with the biggest teeth: They were a foot long!

Tyrannosaurus rex Tyrannosaurus rex Tyrannosaurus rex Tyrannosaurus rex

Tyrannosaurus rex Tyrannosaurus

Tyrannosaurus rex

Compsognathus

Compsognathus Compsognathus Compsognathus

The smallest dinosaur: It was the size of a turkey!

The most armored

Stegosaurus

Stegosaurus

dinosaur: It had a bony-plated back!

Parasaurolophus Parasaurolophus Parasaurolophus Parasaurolophus

The loudest dinosaur: Its head had a bony megaphone!

Parasaurolophus

Triceratops

Triceratops Triceratops Triceratops Triceratops Triceratops

Diplodocus Diplodocus Diplodocus Diplodocus Diplodocus Diplodocus

The oddest dinosaur: It had horns on its nose and forehead!

Prehistoric Record

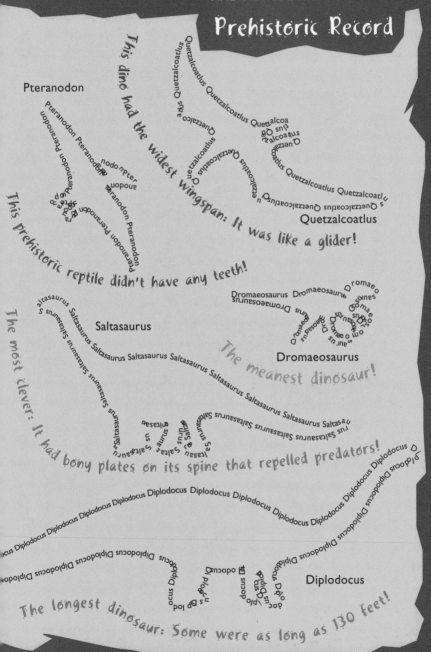

Pteranodon

This dino had the widest wingspan: It was like a glider!

Quetzalcoatlus

This prehistoric reptile didn't have any teeth!

Saltasaurus

Dromaeosaurus

The meanest dinosaur!

The most clever: It had bony plates on its spine that repelled predators!

Diplodocus

The longest dinosaur: Some were as long as 130 feet!

He **tilted** his head and looked up at me as though he didn't understand. His eyes were so **sweet** and innocent that I couldn't just leave him.

"Oh, okay," I said. "I'll take care of you, little guy. First, you need a name. How about **TOPS**?"

Tops nodded. The early morning air was chilly, and Tops was **shivering** from the cold. So I covered him with my jacket, and he soon fell asleep in the nest.

I leaned back and was about to doze off myself when someone pinched my tail and shrieked in my ear: "**HERBIVOROUS** or **carnivorous**? **HERBIVOROUS** or **carnivorous**? **HERBIVOROUS** or **carnivorous**?"

PREHISTORY

TRICERATOPS

Size: Up to twenty-nine feet long
Found: North America
Distinguishing Characteristics: This herbivorous dinosaur lived during the end of the Cretaceous period. Its name means "three-horned face" because of its large horns and bony frill. Triceratops lived in herds.

TRICERATOPS STEW?

"If I'd been carnivorous, you'd be **DEAD** by now!" my cousin Trap said with a chuckle.

I couldn't believe it! I'd never been so glad to see my cousin. And he wasn't **alone** — Professor von Volt, Thea, and Benjamin were there, too!

"I'm so **happy** to see all of you!" I exclaimed.

Professor von Volt explained that he was able to recall the **MOUSE MOVER 3000** with a special **EMERGENCY**  telecommand.

I told him all about my adventures in the Jurassic period.

Benjamin and Tops became instant **FRIENDS**.

Benjamin and Tops became instant friends!

But Trap eyed the adorable dinosaur with HUNGRY eyes.

"I know what we're having for dinner tonight," Trap announced. "We'll have Triceratops stew. Yummy!"

"Don't even think about it!" I scolded Trap. "He's my friend. We can make a vegetable soup instead."

I looked at the plant life around me, and I recognized some modern plants, like oak, magnolias, papyrus, and water lilies. Surely we could find at least a few that were EDIBLE.

Suddenly, Trap got a mischievous glint in his eye.

"Okay, Cuz," he said. "Veggie stew it is. You just leave everything up to me."

I Could Have
Become Extinct!

While Trap worked on dinner, Thea, the professor, and I built a little WOODEN hut on top of a tree branch to protect us from PREHISTORIC snakes and insects.

A few hours later, Trap called me over. He lifted the lid on a pot of soup that was bubbling over the fire. It smelled DELICIOUS!

"Taste it," Trap urged me. "Tell me truthfully what you think. I trust you!"

FLATTERED, I tasted a spoonful of soup.

"So?" Trap asked. "Do you like it?"

"It's good."

He stared at me.

"You feel fine?"

"Of course! Why wouldn't I?"

"Okay, soup's on!" Trap yelled. "LET'S EAT!"

"What's in the soup?" I asked distractedly.

"Some Little prehistoric **MUSHROOMS**!" Trap replied.

"You tested them on me?" I squeaked. "I could have been **poisoned**! I could have gone extinct!"

"Well, **what** was I supposed to put in the pot?" Trap whined. "You wouldn't let me **EAT** the Triceratops!"

THE DINOSAURS' SECRET

The following morning we got up at **dawn** and had breakfast.

Trap made us tea using the leaves of a prehistoric plant, and **scrambled** prehistoric bird eggs spiced with a wild root that tasted like onion.

While we ate, Professor von Volt explained our **mission** to us.

"Dear friends," he began. "We don't know whether the dinosaurs became **extinct** slowly over time or whether it happened more rapidly. But more important, we don't know **WHY** it happened. We're here now to gather the data to help us **UNDERSTAND**. Here are the various hypotheses. . . ."

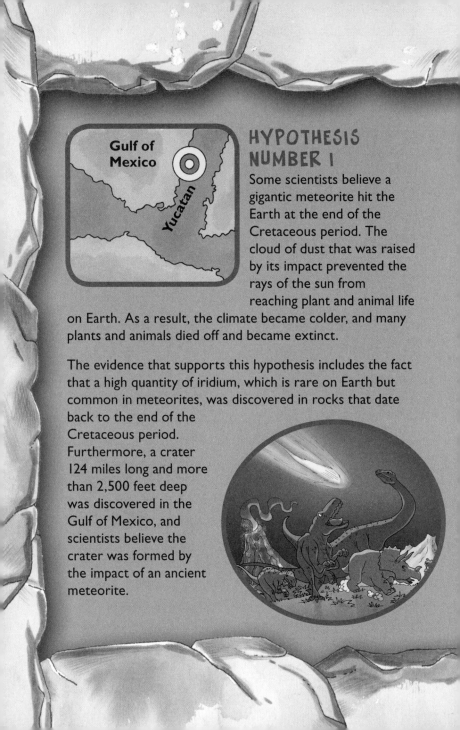

Gulf of Mexico

Yucatan

HYPOTHESIS NUMBER 1

Some scientists believe a gigantic meteorite hit the Earth at the end of the Cretaceous period. The cloud of dust that was raised by its impact prevented the rays of the sun from reaching plant and animal life on Earth. As a result, the climate became colder, and many plants and animals died off and became extinct.

The evidence that supports this hypothesis includes the fact that a high quantity of iridium, which is rare on Earth but common in meteorites, was discovered in rocks that date back to the end of the Cretaceous period. Furthermore, a crater 124 miles long and more than 2,500 feet deep was discovered in the Gulf of Mexico, and scientists believe the crater was formed by the impact of an ancient meteorite.

HYPOTHESIS NUMBER 2

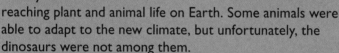

Some scientists believe a climatic change at the end of the Cretaceous period — perhaps one caused by a gigantic volcanic eruption — covered the Earth with lava and smoke. The cloud of ash from the eruption prevented the rays of the sun from reaching plant and animal life on Earth. Some animals were able to adapt to the new climate, but unfortunately, the dinosaurs were not among them.

HYPOTHESIS NUMBER 3

At the end of the Cretaceous period, mammals began to thrive. Some scientists believe these mammals competed with dinosaurs for food and also fed on dinosaur eggs, which may have helped bring on the dinosaurs' extinction!

GOOD-BYE, FRIEND

I took a walk by the river, and thought about Professor von Volt's theories. I took a breath of clean, fresh prehistoric air and felt truly **grateful**. I had been reunited with my family, and was no longer **lost in time**! I felt so peaceful!

I returned to my friends, where we saw a herd of **Triceratops** drinking in the river.

How peaceful!

"When you get BIG, you'll look like them," I told Tops. "You're a Triceratops, not a mouse. Be BRAVE and go join them!"

He hid shyly behind me and shook his head. I gently pushed him toward the group of Triceratops. Tentatively, he approached the herd. Each dinosaur sniffed little Tops, and then they made room for him. They had accepted him!

"Good-bye, little friend!" I called out as the herd walked away. "I will never FORGET you!"

A Living, Breathing Hang Glider!

We worked hard the entire day to collect as much information about the dinosaurs as we could.

At the end of the day, we stopped to rest in a forest of **EUCALYPTUS TREES**. While the others were putting up camp, I took a pail and went to the creek to get some **water**. Suddenly, I heard a terrible screech.

"Grrraaauuukkkkk!"

It was a **HUGE** flying reptile. It had an enormouse sharp, pointed beak, and each wing was more than ten feet wide! It looked like a living, breathing hang glider!

Eucalyptus leaf

"It's the largest prehistoric flying reptile!" Professor von Volt whispered from behind me.

QUETZALCOATLUS

Size: Up to a fifty-foot wingspan
Found: North America
Distinguishing Characteristics: These flying reptiles lived during the Cretaceous period and ate fish. They could not take off from a level place because they were too heavy. Instead, they would launch from a slope and take advantage of the warm winds to carry them gliding through the air.

"QUETZALCOATLUS!"

He pointed to the creature's claw, which was caught in a thorny bush.

"Chances are it won't be able to free itself!" the professor said.

The reptile cried out again in pain, fear, and ANGER.

"Poor thing!" I murmured. "I'll help you!"

"Be careful, Geronimo," the professor warned me. "A wounded animal is always dangerous!"

I slowly reached over to cut the THORNY branches with a knife. A moment later, the creature's paw was freed. He stared at me for a few seconds. Then he climbed to the top of a eucalyptus tree and launched into the air.

HERE, DINO, DINO, DINO!

We packed up our camp and continued our **journey** the next day. I noticed something was following us in the air: It was the **Quetzalcoatlus** I had saved! I waved at it, and the reptile replied by **dipping** his head as if to say thank you before he flew away. It was an **INCREDIBLE** moment.

Then just a second later, I stubbed my toe on a fossil.

"**YEOW!**" I shouted. So much for my incredible moment!

I reached down to pick up an **AMAZING** fossilized fern leaf.

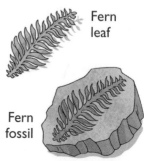

Fern leaf

Fern fossil

Fossils are the preserved remains of plants or animals that lived millions of years ago. Fossils are useful to scientists because they help them reconstruct prehistoric environments.

"**LOOK!**" I showed Benjamin. "It's a fern fossil."

"Wow!" Benjamin exclaimed, looking up at me admiringly. "That's so cool, Uncle G."

"Well, Benjamin," Trap broke in, "if you think that's **cool**, look at this!"

Trap pointed to a small dinosaur with **BRIGHTLY COLORED**, scaly skin. It had long, sharp claws, and looked mean. As soon as the dinosaur saw Trap, a **Second** dinosaur sprung up behind it, and then a **third** dinosaur emerged from a clump of ferns. Soon, a **fourth, fifth, Sixth, Seventh**, and **eighth** dinosaur appeared! Holey cheese — there were a lot of them!

"Here, dino, dino, dino," Trap cooed to the **first** dinosaur.

"Uh, Trap," I warned, "I wouldn't do that. I'm getting a **BAD** feeling here. A very, very, very bad feeling!"

I quickly grabbed the *Time Travel Survival Manual* and frantically leafed through it. **HORRIFIED**, I began to read aloud:

"'The **Dromaeosaurus** is a small **carnivorous** dinosaur that hunts in packs.'"

Trap shrugged.

"So what?" he asked. "Come on, these little guys are as **sweet** as puppies. Isn't that right?"

Trap cooed at the dinosaurs again.

"Trap, I **REALLY** wouldn't —" I began, but Trap cut me off.

"You're such a **scaredy-mouse**, Geronimo!" Trap scoffed. "Let me show you. Here, dino, dino, dino. Come to Uncle Trap!"

He stretched out his arm and offered the little dinosaur a mushroom.

The dinosaur sniffed at the mushroom but then decided he would rather try a bite of Trap's tasty-looking finger. "YEOOOOW!" Trap cried.

I grabbed a bone and **waved** it in the air.

"Go away!" I shouted at the little Dromaeosaurus.

"Come any closer, and I'll make dinosaur **MEATBALLS** out

of you!" Trap added, waving a bone he had found as well.

But the dinosaur seemed to like the **taste** it had gotten of Trap's finger.

Suddenly, the pack **ATTACKED** all at once. They threw Trap on the ground, and one of them grabbed his arm with its sharp fangs. Who knows what would have happened if I hadn't **FURIOUSLY** waved the bone and shouted at the top of my lungs.

"**GO AWAYYYYYYYYYYY!**" I yelled. "Scram!"

Taken by surprise, the Dromaeosaurs retreated and **swiftly** took flight.

Aaaaaahhhhh!

Poor Trap was as pale as a slice of mozzarella. I would have been, too, if the Dromaeosaurus had grabbed my arm.

"G-Geronimo . . ." Trap mumbled.

"What?" I asked.

He pointed to something **behind** me.

"G-Geronimo . . . the ty-ty-ty . . ."

"What is it, Trap?" I urged him **bravely**. "Don't worry, I'll protect you!"

"Behind you!" he shrieked. "Turn around!"

I turned and found myself face-to-face with a

TYRANNOSAURUS REX!

PREHISTORY

TYRANNOSAURUS REX
Size: Up to forty feet long and thirteen feet tall
Found: North America
Distinguishing Characteristics: This carnivorous dinosaur lived at the end of the Cretaceous period. Its name means "tyrant lizard." It had a gigantic skull, short two-fingered arms, strong jaws, and long, sharp serrated teeth.

I'M AFRAID OF
HEIGHTS!

Benjamin, smart little mouse that he is, had **climbed** to the top of a eucalyptus tree when the Dromaeosaurs attacked.

"Uncle Geronimo!" he shouted from the tree. "The Tyrannosaurus rex is **carnivorous**. Ruuuun!"

I **RAN** and **RAN** until I was out of breath. The T. rex's huge footsteps echoed through the forest, and the ground shook under its weight!

The T. rex was huge. I wasn't going to win this battle unless I used my wits! Then I had an idea. Right in front of me was a deep gorge with a **narrow** rock bridge over it. The bridge would hold my weight, but it would **collapse** under the weight of the T. rex! I scampered across, trying not to look down. I'm afraid of heights!

Once I got to the other side, the rock began to **crumble**, and the T. rex fell with a growl. But now how was I going to get back to the other side? Then I heard the **rustling** of wings. It was the Quetzalcoatlus!

"Please help me!" I **BEGGED**.

A second later, he allowed me to climb up onto his wings. Then he **gently** carried me back to my friends. Touched, I gave him a **BIG** hug.

This is the **secret** to real friendship: Support each other and try to always be there when a **friend** is in need!

THE VOICE OF THE PREHISTORIC FOREST

By the time I was reunited with my friends, **night** had fallen. Thea, who is an expert in survival techniques, rubbed two pieces of flint together. She used the **SPARK** to ignite some dried leaves. Then she slowly added pieces of bark, twigs, and large logs until we had a **BRIGHT**, burning fire.

She found five branches shaped like **FORKS** and carved five pieces of wood into **spoons** for all of us. Then she served up some soup she had made in a carved-out gourd!

I offered to take my turn as the night watch. The light from the fire threw eerie **shadows** on the cave walls. Outside the cave, I heard the voices of the forest — strange calls, growls, and funny cries echoed in the night.

How terrifying! Would we survive in the **wild** forest of the Cretaceous period? I **shivered** and held on to the Giganotosaurus bone I had used to fend off the herd of Dromaeosaurus.

The next day, we picked up rock samples, took photos of plants and animals, and jotted down INVALUABLE notes. We were learning so much about the evolution of life.

"I have an **ANNOUNCEMENT**," the professor said. "We've collected enough information to complete our mission in prehistoric times. If everyone agrees, we can leave **tomorrow**. Let's have a show of paws."

We all raised our **paws** at the same time.

Then Trap cleared his throat. "I have an **announcement** as well," he said. "To

celebrate the **greatest cook in the world** — by which I mean me — I'd like to prepare a **SPECIAL PREHISTORIC MENU** tonight," Trap told us.

"Now, let's see . . . I brought all of the cheeses from home, but I'll need help getting all of the other supplies," Trap said.

He handed me a **LOOOOOOOOOOOOONG** list of ingredients to find.

"Here's what I need, Cuz," he said, giving me a

Evolution of life from the first life-forms of the sea to primates

One of the first multicellular beings

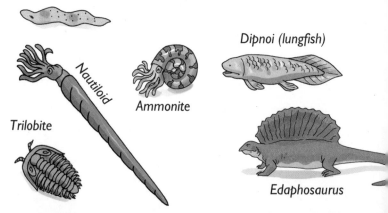

Dipnoi (lungfish)

Nautiloid

Ammonite

Trilobite

Edaphosaurus

little shove. "Hop to it!"

Holey cheese . . . there were some **strange** things on that list! Snails, breadfruit, algae, freshly shucked mollusks, sturgeon, hearts of palm, and figs. Where, oh, where was I going to find all this **STUFF**?

Luckily, Professor von Volt offered to **HELP**.

"Don't worry, Geronimo," he told me. "I know exactly where we can get everything. **LET'S GO!**"

Pteranodon

Stegosaurus

Plateosaurus

Saber-toothed tiger

Primate

A LAKE, A SUNSET, AND TWO TRUE FRIENDS

Professor von Volt and I headed for the lake. As we walked, he pointed out all sorts of **AMAZING** specimens of plant and animal life to me. It was incredible!

When we got to the lake, the professor pulled a **NET** out of his backpack. Then he showed me how to scoop and strain algae. While I **harvested** the algae, he began hunting for snails.

BLECH!

That algae was so slippery and **slimy**, and it smelled awful! In fact, it had the most **TERRIBLE** stench! I really hoped Trap's **WORLD-FAMOUSE** recipe

SALTASAURUS

Size: Up to thirty-nine feet long
Found: South America
Distinguishing Characteristics:
This herbivorous dinosaur lived at the end of the Cretaceous period. Its body was armored with bony plates that were embedded in its skin.

would make it taste better than it smelled.

As I scooped the algae, I suddenly noticed a dinosaur with a very

LOOOOOOOONG neck just a few feet away from me. It was a **Saltasaurus**!

I immediately knew it was herbivorous because it was happily munching on the juiciest buds on a very **TALL** poplar tree.

"Splendid, isn't it?" Professor von Volt asked.

"**Nature** is life's greatest treasure!"

I nodded in agreement, **AWESTRUCK** by the sight of the enormouse dinosaur.

"Dearest Geronimo, there's something that's been weighing on me," the professor continued. "I've been thinking about **extinction**.

"Whenever a species dies out, it's **TRAGIC**," Professor von Volt explained. "Many species — like the DINOSAURS — became extinct during prehistoric times. But even today, animals like tigers, whales, and pandas are at RISK. The destruction of these animals' natural habitats, hunting, and pollution all contribute to the problem."

He shook his head. "The natural equilibrium of nature needs to be *respected*! Nature is WiSeR than we think."

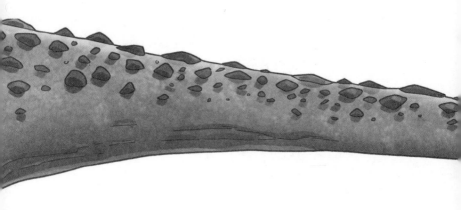

We sat on the bank of the prehistoric lake, dangling our paws in the water. A lake, a PINK sunset, and true friendship. What more could a mouse ask for?

Professor von Volt and I brought Trap the ingredients we had gathered. He stood at the fire and sang while he worked.

A tiny Compsognathus came nosing around trying to STEAL some of Trap's food. At first, Trap SHOOED the DINOSAUR away, but then he SOFTENED and threw him a little morsel.

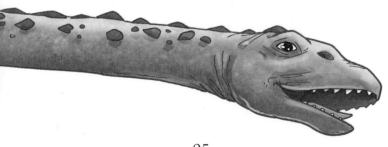

COMPSOGNATHUS

Size: About three feet long
Found: Europe
Distinguishing Characteristics: This tiny carnivorous dinosaur lived at the end of the Jurassic period. Its name means "graceful jaw." It was one of the smallest dinosaurs, and it fed on worms and small lizards.

"Here's a little **MEAT**," Trap whispered. "You should have a good meal tonight, too!"

Trap was true to his word — our dinner was **delicious**! We went to sleep feeling full and **HaPPY**.

But at five in the morning, the earth began to

shake!

METEORITES!

I woke up with a start and saw hundreds of meteorites streaking across the sky.

"METEORITES!" Professor von Volt shouted. "The dinosaurs might be about to go extinct!"

There was **CHAOS** all around us. Herds of terrorized dinosaurs galloped through the forest, knocking down shrubs and trees as they fled.

"It's time for us to go to **Egypt** to find out how Cheops — that is, the Great Pyramid of Giza — was built!"

With trembling paws, the professor programmed the Chronometer.

July 16, 1280 BC
Giza

A meteorite **CRASHED** to Earth right next to us! The ground beneath my paws **trembled** forebodingly.

Suddenly, a thick, **smelly**, and slimy black substance rained down on me from above. I looked up to see the tail of a huge dinosaur going by.

"Dinosaur dung!" I squeaked. I tried to wipe it off, but instead I slipped and landed in an even **BIGGER** heap of it! I tried desperately to extract myself, but it was useless. I was stuck!

"Don't worry, Uncle!" Benjamin called.

"We'll pull you out, little brother!" Thea shouted.

Then Thea, Benjamin, and Trap grabbed my tail and pulled me out. Plop!

To wash me off, my cousin threw a bucket of freezing water on my face. SPLASH!

"I want to go **HOOOOOOOOME**!" I sobbed.

We all **jumped** into the time machine.

Professor von Volt checked the chronometer, then pressed the flight button.

"We're not going home yet, Geronimo! Next stop, Egypt!"

The little ship began to vibrate and fill with a BLUE MIST.

I wondered what **FABUMOUSE** adventures we'd find in Egypt. Would we meet a pharoah? Or explore a pyramid? You'll read all about it in my next book — **MOUSE'S honor**.

So farewell until then, dear mouse friends!

Dear rodent friends,

I hope you have enjoyed reading all about my adventures in prehistoric times. To keep the memories from fading, I wrote this very special travel journal just for you. It's full of **definitions**, MAPS, and FUN FACTS.

Learn about paleontology and dinosaur discoveries around the world. You'll find it's like taking off on another fabumouse journey through time!

Geronimo Stilton

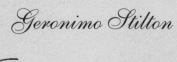

PREHISTORY
MINI DICTIONARY

carnivore: An animal that eats meat.

bird: A warm-blooded animal with two legs, wings, feathers, and a beak. The oldest known bird is Archaeopteryx, which lived in the Late Jurassic period around 150 million years ago.

egg: An oval or round object that contains a baby bird, reptile, fish, or insect. It is produced by the female member of these species to protect their young as they develop. Dinosaurs laid eggs in nests. The largest dinosaur eggs were as big as eighteen or nineteen inches long, while the smallest were the size of tennis balls.

family: A group of living things that are related to each other. Donkeys and mules are members of the horse family.

genus: A group of related plants or animals that is larger than a species but smaller than a family.

herbivore: An animal that only eats plants.

mammal: A warm-blooded animal that has hair or fur and usually gives birth to live babies. Female mammals produce milk to feed their young.

paleontology: The science that deals with fossils and other ancient life forms. A person who studies paleontology is called a paleontologist.

prehistory: A time before history was recorded in written form.

reptile: A cold-blooded animal that crawls across the ground or creeps on short legs. Most reptiles have backbones and reproduce by laying eggs.

species: One of the groups into which animals and plants of the same genus are divided. Members of the same species can mate and have offspring.

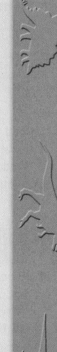

DINOSAURS AROUND THE WORLD

England: In 1841, Sir Richard Owen coined the term *dinosaur*, which means "terrible lizard."

United States: Visitors to Dinosaur National Monument on the border of Colorado and Utah can view a wall of approximately 1,500 dinosaur bones and touch real 149-million-year-old dinosaur fossils!

Morocco: The Kem Kem Formation is a geological formation that dates to the Late Cretaceous period. Many dinosaur fossils have been discovered there.

Argentina: In 1993, an amateur fossil hunter named Rubén Dario Carolini discovered the most complete Giganotosaurus fossil in the Candeleros formation in Patagonia.

Italy: In 1981, the first dinosaur fossil ever found in Italy is the only known fossil of Scipionyx, a bipedal predator whose body was most likely covered by primitive feathers. The fossil is unique because it contained several petrified internal organs, including intestines that contained half-digested meals of lizards and fish.

Mongolia: In 1924, a skeleton and fossilized eggs in a nest were discovered in the Gobi Desert in Mongolia. Scientists initially thought the dinosaur was stealing the eggs, and they gave it the name Oviraptor (meaning "egg thief"). It was later discovered that the skeleton had been a parent watching over its own nest of eggs.

China: Mamenchisaurus — the largest Asiatic dinosaur and the dinosaur with the longest neck — was first discovered in 1952 in Sichuan, China.

Australia: The bones of the largest dinosaurs ever discovered in Australia are those of two sauropods nicknamed Cooper and George, found in 2005 and 2006.

Fun Facts

The dinosaur that . . .

Was the fastest: Dromiceiomimus could run at a speed of around thirty-seven miles per hour.

Was the heaviest: Argentinosaurus weighed around eighty tons.

Was the tallest: Sauroposeidon's head could reach fifty-seven feet in height.

Had the longest neck: Mamenchisaurus's neck made up half its length.

Had the longest tail: Diplodocus's tail was up to forty-five feet long.

Had the longest name: Micropachycephalosaurus

Was the first discovered: Megalosaurus was discovered and named in 1824.

Don't miss my next journey through time!

PYRAMID PUZZLE

Our second time-traveling adventure was in ancient Egypt. We were there to discover how the Great Pyramid of Giza was built. But when we arrived, we were arrested by the Grand Vizier, and taken to see the pharaoh — who threw us in the dungeon! Would we be able to escape, or would we be fed to the crocodiles?

Be sure to read these stories, too!

#1 Lost Treasure of the Emerald Eye

#2 The Curse of the Cheese Pyramid

#3 Cat and Mouse in a Haunted House

#4 I'm Too Fond of My Fur!

#5 Four Mice Deep in the Jungle

#6 Paws Off, Cheddarface!

#7 Red Pizzas for a Blue Count

#8 Attack of the Bandit Cats

#9 A Fabumouse Vacation for Geronimo

#10 All Because of a Cup of Coffee

#11 It's Halloween, You 'Fraidy Mouse!

#12 Merry Christmas, Geronimo!

#13 The Phantom of the Subway

#14 The Temple of the Ruby of Fire

#15 The Mona Mousa Code

#16 A Cheese-Colored Camper

#17 Watch Your Whiskers, Stilton!

#18 Shipwreck on the Pirate Islands

#19 My Name Is Stilton, Geronimo Stilton

#20 Surf's Up, Geronimo!

#21 The Wild, Wild West

#22 The Secret of Cacklefur Castle

A Christmas Tale

#23 Valentine's Day Disaster

#24 Field Trip to Niagara Falls

#25 The Search for Sunken Treasure

#26 The Mummy with No Name

#27 The Christmas Toy Factory

#28 Wedding Crasher

#29 Down and Out Down Under

#30 The Mouse Island Marathon

#31 The Mysterious Cheese Thief

Christmas Catastrophe

#32 Valley of the Giant Skeletons

#33 Geronimo and the Gold Medal Mystery

#34 Geronimo Stilton, Secret Agent

#35 A Very Merry Christmas

#36 Geronimo's Valentine

#37 The Race Across America

#38 A Fabumouse School Adventure

#39 Singing Sensation

#40 The Karate Mouse

#41 Mighty Mount Kilimanjaro

#42 The Peculiar Pumpkin Thief

#43 I'm Not a Supermouse!

#44 The Giant Diamond Robbery

#45 Save the White Whale!

#46 The Haunted Castle

#47 Run for the Hills, Geronimo!

#48 The Mystery in Venice

#49 The Way of the Samurai

#50 This Hotel Is Haunted!

#51 The Enormouse Pearl Heist

#52 Mouse in Space!

#53 Rumble in the Jungle

#54 Get into Gear, Stilton!

#55 The Golden Statue Plot

#56 Flight of the Red Bandit